Written by Jillian Harker
Illustrated by Gill McLean

This edition published by Parragon in 2010
Parragon
Queen Street House
4 Queen Street
Bath BA1 1HE, UK

Copyright © Parragon Books Ltd 2009

ISBN 978-1-4075-6371-8

Printed in China

I Wish...

Bath · New York · Singapore · Hong Kong · Cologne · Delhi · Melbourne

Benji sat on the bed, feeling a little bit lonely. He was new here, and he hadn't seen anyone else in the bedroom.

He watched a moonbeam slip through a gap in the curtains and slide across the bed.

"I wish I had someone to play with," he whispered.

"Did I hear someone say they wanted to play?" asked a voice. The lid of the toy box flew open, and out climbed a dangly-legged, spotted horse.
"Hi, I'm Dottie… and I love to play!"

Boing!

Boing!

Dottie jumped onto the bed and began to bounce up and down.

"Where did you come from?" she asked.

"From the birthday party," replied Benji. "I was a present."

"Did someone mention a party?" A friendly-looking monkey poked his head around the curtain. "Why weren't Rosie and I invited?"

A floppy-eared rabbit appeared beside him. "Max and I love parties!" Rosie the rabbit told Benji. "And so does Humph."

She stared at the toy box. A loud yawn came from inside. Then a bright blue hippo slowly lifted his head.

Party!

"A party!" said Humph. "That means food. And I'm hungry! Is there anything left to eat?"

"I think there are some cupcakes in the kitchen," replied Benji. "But do you think we should…?"

But Humph was already
out the door!

"Oh!" said Benji, looking at the
other toys. "Should we go after him?"

Benji was bumping down the
stairs after Humph when Dottie
zoomed past.
"This is fun!" she neighed.
"Wait for me!" called Benji.

WHEEEE!

In the kitchen, Humph was about to take a bite out of a leftover cupcake. The candle was already halfway into his mouth.

Benji grabbed it just in time.
"Excuse me," he explained, "but
you aren't supposed to eat that part."
"Thanks, Benji. You're smart.
I wish I knew things like that,"
grumbled Humph.

Before Benji could explain about the candle, he heard Dottie and Rosie yell loudly. They were staring at a large black shape outside the kitchen window.

They grabbed Benji and held on tight.

"It's just a cat," Benji said. "No need to worry."
"Phew," sighed Rosie with relief.
"I wish I could be as brave as you, Benji," laughed Dottie.

"That cat will stay outside, won't it?" whispered Max. They all looked to Benji for reassurance. Max had crept across the room and hidden under the table. Humph's knees were shaking.

There was a squeaking noise and then a loud **clatter!**

"Don't worry, that's just the cat coming into the kitchen," explained Benji. But Humph and Dottie, Max and Rosie had all raced out through the kitchen door and disappeared up the stairs as fast as their legs could carry them!

Benji found them all back in the
bedroom. It took some time to persuade
them to come out.

"Benji, will you always be here
to look after us?" Dottie asked him.

Benji gave a tiny little smile. It was
nice to feel wanted.

"Of course," he replied.

Humph was tired from their adventure. "How am I going to sleep when I'm so hungry?" he sniffed, settling back down on the bed.

Dottie and Rosie giggled. They danced around on the bed. Max joined in.

"Why don't we all play in the yard tomorrow?"
Rosie suggested.
"What's your yard like?" asked Benji.
"I'll show you," said Dottie, and she helped Benji
up so he could look out the window.

"Wow!" he said. "It looks really exciting.
Are you going to play in the yard, Humph?"

"Humph!" said Humph sleepily. "It's such a long
way to the yard. I might just take a little nap instead."

Benji smiled at his sleepy new friend.

Dottie jumped back onto the bed and started to bounce. Benji looked up at the moon. He had a feeling that he wouldn't be lonely anymore.

"I wish that tomorrow is as much fun as today," he whispered.

Then Benji turned to
his new friends and took
a huge leap, and began
to bounce on the bed.
"Here's to friends!"
he laughed.